GENERATOR REX

CN CARTOON NETWORK.

EVOS and HEROES

By Billy Wrecks

A GOLDEN BOOK · NEW YORK

GENERATOR REX, CARTOON NETWORK, the logos, and all related characters and e...
© 2011 Cartoon Network. All rights reserved. Published in the United States b...
Random House Children's Books, a division of Random House, Inc., 1745 Broad...
Golden Books, A Golden Book, and the G colophon are registered trademark...

ISBN: 978-0-375-87378-2
www.randomhouse.com/kids

REX

Rex is like any other teenager—except he has the totally awesome ability to generate living machine parts from his body! His powers come in handy because he lives in a world infected with tiny robots called nanites that can cause living creatures to mutate into horrible monsters called Evos.

Rex not only uses his powers to stop Evos in their tracks, he can also cure the mutated humans and return them to normal. That's a big responsibility for a young hero—even one as cool as Rex!

Rex is troubled by the fact that he has no memory of his past. He can never be sure who are his real friends—or foes!

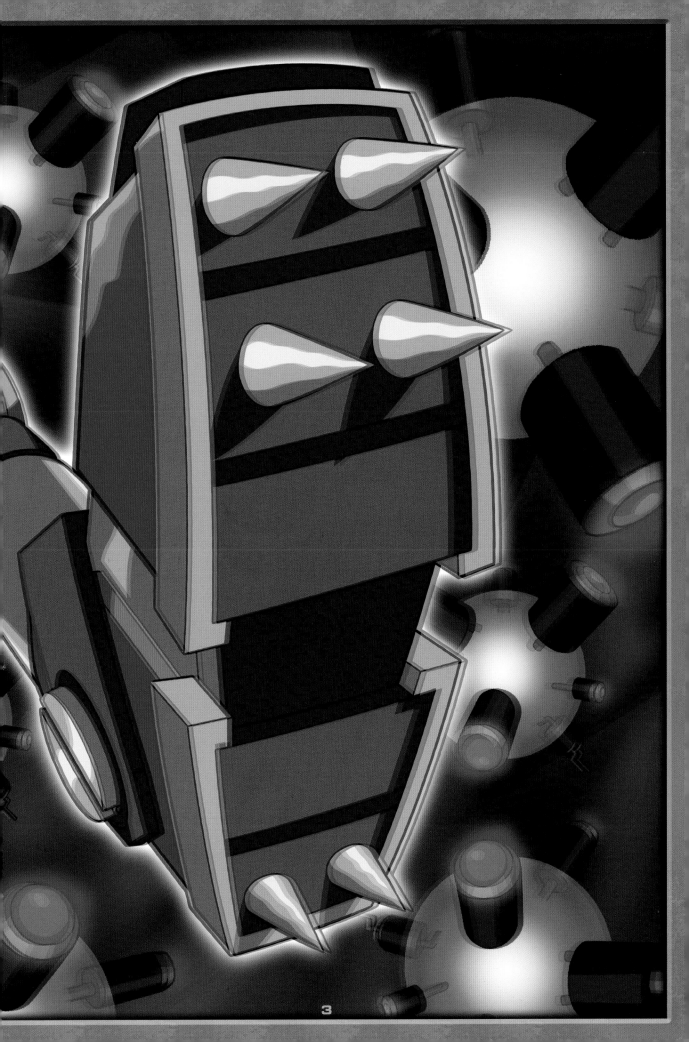

SMACKHANDS

Rex uses his oversized fists to bring down even the biggest Evos—and some of them get really big!

PUNKBUSTERS

What a kick! Evos run when Rex starts stomping in his massive Punkbuster boots.

HOVERBIKE

Getting around is not a problem for Rex. He can fly with his Boogie Pack—or take a high-speed ride on a hoverbike that grows right out of his legs!

SLAM CANNON

When Rex has to bring out the big guns, he uses his Slam Cannon. It fires cannonball-like projectiles that blast through everything in their path and take the fight out of any Evo.

BOBO HAHA

He may have a bad attitude and a preference for the easy life, but Bobo Haha is Rex's best friend and sidekick. Armed with a pair of powerful blasters and a stylish fez, this talking chimp is always ready to put Evos in their place.

AGENT SIX

Agent Six is the no-nonsense leader of Rex's missions against out-of-control Evos. Skilled in several martial arts, Agent Six is more than a match for the dangers he and Rex encounter. With two swords called katanas that deploy from his sleeves, he can slice through almost anything that gets in his way—and Agent Six doesn't like it when things get in his way.

Rex is in the care of Providence, an organization of scientists and soldiers dedicated to controlling the threat of Evos. Providence is led by a mysterious figure known only as the White Knight, who will resort to any means necessary to rid the world of nanites. Even though Rex and Agent Six are the first line of defense against Evos, Captain Calen and Providence's team of elite agents are always ready to provide backup with plenty of muscle, high-tech gear, and amazing vehicles.

VAN KLEISS

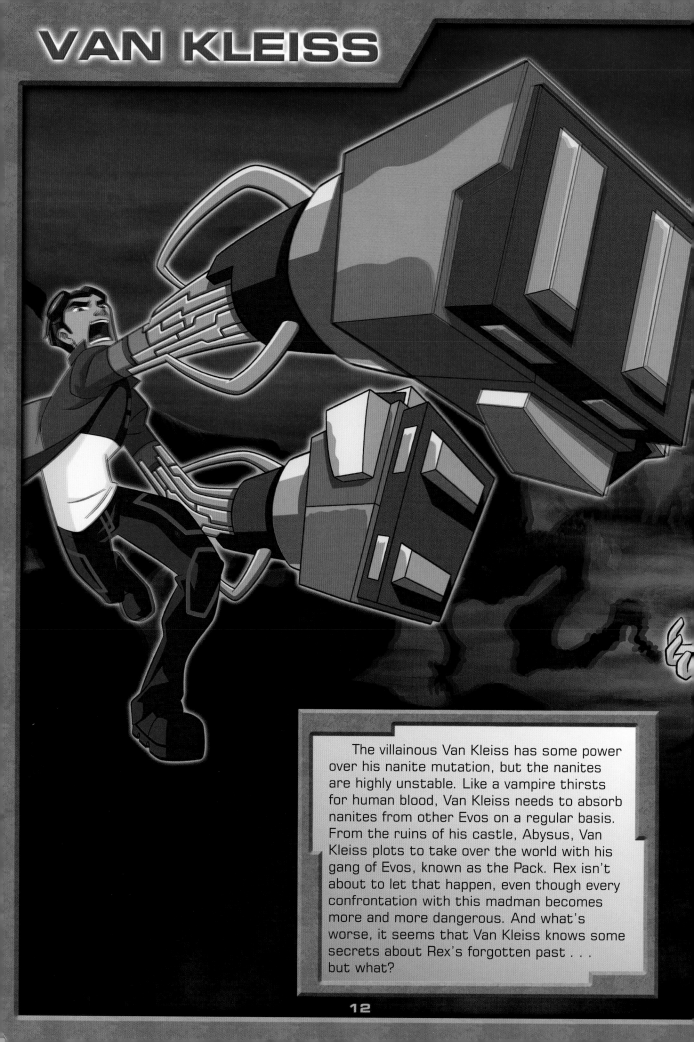

The villainous Van Kleiss has some power over his nanite mutation, but the nanites are highly unstable. Like a vampire thirsts for human blood, Van Kleiss needs to absorb nanites from other Evos on a regular basis. From the ruins of his castle, Abysus, Van Kleiss plots to take over the world with his gang of Evos, known as the Pack. Rex isn't about to let that happen, even though every confrontation with this madman becomes more and more dangerous. And what's worse, it seems that Van Kleiss knows some secrets about Rex's forgotten past . . . but what?

BREACH

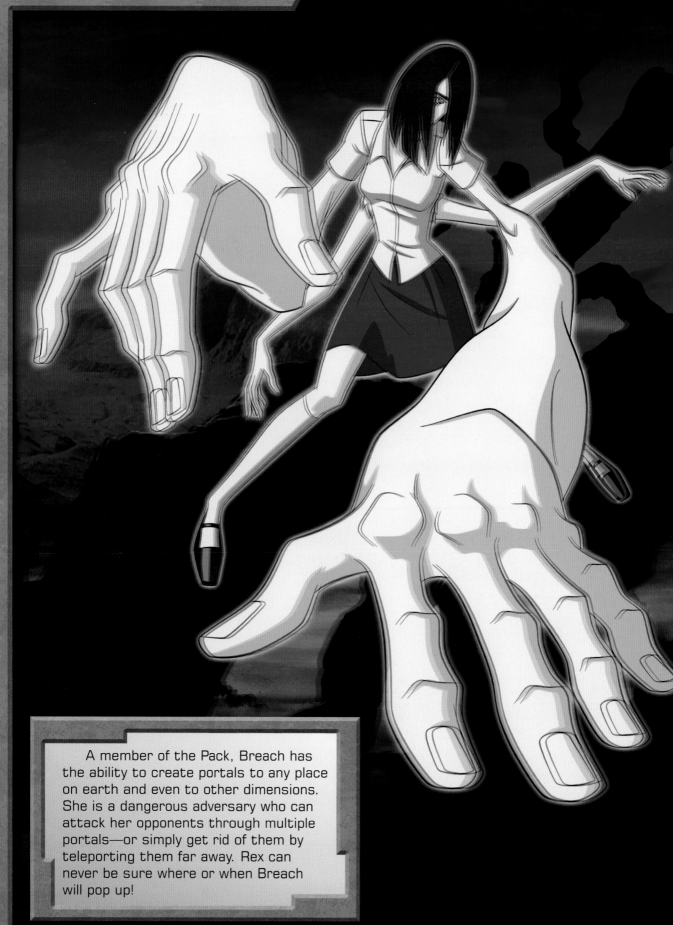

A member of the Pack, Breach has the ability to create portals to any place on earth and even to other dimensions. She is a dangerous adversary who can attack her opponents through multiple portals—or simply get rid of them by teleporting them far away. Rex can never be sure where or when Breach will pop up!

Van Kleiss's henchman is Biowulf, a strange amalgam of robot armor and snarling werewolf. Biowulf has amazing speed and strength, plus long, razor-sharp claws on each hand. Rex keeps his guard up when he faces this formidable foe.

SKALAMANDER

Skalamander is a large reptilian Evo with jagged rocks growing out of his slimy green body. His left fist is like a stone club, and he uses it to smash anything that gets too close. Rex keeps his distance from this misshapen Evo, but Skalamander can also fire sharp, daggerlike crystals out of his body with lethal accuracy!